MOVING ON

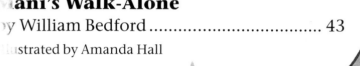

Rigby is an imprint of Pearson Education Limited, a company incorporated in England and Wales, having its registered office at Edinburgh Gate, Harlow, Essex, CM20 2JE.
Registered company number: 872828
www.rigbyed.co.uk

Rigby is a registered trademark of Reed Elsevier Inc, Licensed to Pearson Education Limited

Moving On first published 2002

Series editor: Wendy Wren

11
12

Moving On   ISBN 978 0433 07855 5
Group Reading Pack with Teaching Notes   ISBN 978 0433 07861 6

Illustrated by Martin Cottam, Christine Ross, Amanda Hall
Cover illustration © Steve May 2002
Repro by Digital Imaging, Glasgow
Printed in China (CTPS/12)

All's Well That Ends Well

by Mick Gowar

A small town in Warwickshire, 1579

Thwack!

Dickon flinched as the master's hand smashed down onto the top of the desk. Every other boy in the twilight world of the wood-panelled schoolroom flinched, too.

"Stupid, idle boy! Have you learned nothing – *nothing* – since you came to this school? You there, Master William … Yes, you! Put us out of our misery. Tell us … " The schoolmaster's arm, like a crow's wing in the broad sleeve of his black gown, swept around the room in a theatrical gesture. "What happened to King Midas next?"

Will looked at all the faces turned towards him: the schoolmaster's, a mixture of anger and frustration; the other boys', full of contempt and loathing.

"Translate!" bellowed the master.

Will stared down at the page of Latin. "The god of Delos … stretched out … his ears," he began hesitantly. "I th-think that must mean King Midas' ears, not the god of Delos … "

"Yes, yes, quite," said Master Cottom. "Continue."

"He covered them with shaggy grey hair, and made them twist and turn at the base. He gave them powers of movement. Though the rest of him was human, Midas now wore the ears of a slow-moving donkey. He was anxious to conceal them, and tried to ... "

"Yes, yes! That's enough." The master turned from Will to Dickon. "That is how it should be done. Stand up!"

Dickon got slowly to his feet and turned to face the class. As the master picked up the bunch of birch twigs from the floor, the boy glared at Will. He mouthed three words: I'll get you!

"Bend over the bench."

The boy bent forwards. The master raised the birch and took aim. There was a moment's silence, then, *Thwack!*

Will walked as slowly as he could down the gloomy corridor towards the great oak door that led to the world outside, a world where Dickon would be waiting behind a bush or a tree with a very big stick in his hand. He shouldered open the heavy door and peered around it. Good. There was no sign of Dickon, or anyone else. Trying to look confident, Will strolled across the school-yard to the gate in the far corner.

He felt scared, but angry too. It wasn't fair! It wasn't his fault that he found the lessons easy, and that the new master always picked on him to give the right answers. Yet all the other pupils seemed to hate him for it. He wasn't to blame. He never volunteered to read or give an answer. He was as much picked on by Master Cottom as Dickon or any of the others.

He didn't mean to do well at his lessons. It was just that he got drawn into any story or poem he was reading. He didn't know how it happened, but whenever he started to read, he could actually see things. It was as if a troop of players were acting it out. Reading the passage that morning in the Latin lesson, he had actually seen vain, stupid King Midas trying to hide his enormous donkey's ears under a hat, and twitching them to avoid the flies.

"Spare a farthing for a poor, sick man, kind sir. Just a farthing."

Will looked down. Staring up at him from the gloom and muck beneath the lowest window of the nearest house was a beggar. He was dressed in ragged breeches and an old torn doublet with only one sleeve.

"Look, kind sir. Take a look!" The man pulled open his doublet. On his chest were three large red marks, like sores. "What do you think to those, kind sir?" he asked, in a voice that sounded almost cheerful. "Them's worth a farthing, ain't they?"

Roughly shaken from his daydreaming, and suddenly faced with the repulsive beggar, Will turned and ran. Down the dark narrow street he hurtled, dodging the piles of rubbish and filth which had been dumped outside the houses.

He reached the corner of the street, where he stopped and caught his breath for a moment or two. He felt so stupid. *It was only a harmless beggar – nothing to be afraid of,* he thought. He looked around to check if anyone had seen him running away. The street was deserted. Feeling better, Will turned the corner into Sheep Street.

"Well, well – what a surprise!"

A strong hand grabbed Will's collar. He turned, only to find himself gazing up into the face of Dickon. "See who we have here, lads! Why, it's our good friend, young Master Shake-spite."

Will felt heavy hands on his shoulders. He looked round in panic. It was Jack and Hal, friends of Dickon and both big, strong lads. Big, strong lads who had been beaten by the schoolmaster over the last couple of days, following one of Will's reluctant demonstrations.

"So, Master Learned, Master Scholar – Master Traitor!" Dickon continued, with a grin. "We meet again, but this time not in the schoolroom. What bad luck for you! Look around – there's no schoolmaster here to look after you!"

"No schoolmaster to tie the laces of your doublet for you," chimed in Hal.

"Or wipe your nose," added Jack.

"Yes, Master Shake-school!"

"Master Lick-spittle!"

"Master Scum-speare!"

"W-what do you w-want with me?" asked Will.

"Why, Will, we're your good friends! What would we want but the pleasure of your company?" Dickon put his arm tightly around Will's neck. He grinned broadly. His face was so close that Will could smell the onions and stale beer on his breath.

"And like good friends, we're going to take a little walk together, down to the river. I know a stout tree that grows on the bank where three fine lads might cut three fine sticks. And with those sticks they might teach another fellow a lesson or two." He paused, as if deep in thought. "For example: Lesson One might be in keeping his mouth shut. Lesson Two might be in how painful a beating is. A lad who learns those lessons won't be so quick to get other lads beaten. Isn't that true, boys?"

"Yes, Dickon."

"You're right there, Dickon."

Will struggled to loosen Dickon's grip around his neck. But the tight grip of the butcher's son just got tighter. "Now, we don't want you running off Will, and leaving your new friends. Not before we've been able to teach you those useful lessons. So I'll keep a tight hold on you, and so will Hal and Jack." Will felt the heavy hands squeeze his shoulders again. "And there'll be no crying out or — " Dickon's grip tightened further still, and Will gagged. "We wouldn't want our good friend to choke, would we lads?"

"Oh, no, Dickon."

"We wouldn't want that at all."

And off they went down Sheep Street towards Waterside, arm in arm, looking to all the world like four good friends out for fun. Will was terrified. He was on the edge of tears when, quite without warning, rescue came from the last person he might have expected.

"Dickon, my boy!" called out a loud voice from ahead.

Standing on the opposite side of the road was a burly figure in a handsome, fur-trimmed gown. It was Richard Ford, Dickon's father. He bustled across the road to where the four boys were standing. "Off for some sport, eh, lads?"

"Aye, Father," replied Dickon cheerfully.

"Good, good," said Master Ford. "And here's young Will with you! I'm very glad to see you lads are getting along so well, because we'll be seeing a lot more of young Will from now on – a lot more. I'm sorry to break up this jolly little party, but I think Will should go home as fast as he can. His father has something very important to tell him."

Reluctantly, Dickon and the others let go of Will. Muttering prayers of thanks to all the saints he could think of, Will ran through a maze of narrow alleys to Bridge Street, then along Henley Street, as fast as he could. He didn't slow down until he was home. As he walked along the side passage, Will caught the familiar stench of the stagnant pools behind the house, where the hides his father made into gloves lay tanning in sodden piles.

His mother and father were both in the kitchen. His mother was seated at the table gazing mournfully at the spot on the floor where his sister Anne used to sit, dressing her doll and chatting to it while her mother dealt with the housework. *Poor Mother*, thought Will.

It was three months since Anne had died of a fever and his mother was still grieving as bitterly as if it had happened yesterday.

Will's father was leaning on the big oak dresser, also looking far from cheerful. As Will came through the door, his father wobbled slightly, as if Will had knocked him off balance. He had been drinking.

"Ah, Will, dear boy! There you are, my son, there you are." His greeting was too hearty and his speech was slurred.

"Sit down, dear boy. Take a seat." He pointed to a wooden stool beside the cold hearth. Then he turned to Will's mother. "Leave us, Mistress. We have men's business to discuss."

With a fleeting glance at Will, his mother stood up and walked slowly from the kitchen into the parlour beyond.

"I have something important to tell you, Will," said his father. "As you may have seen, things have not been going too well of late … not too well at all. A bit of wool trading I was involved in … well, things went wrong, badly wrong. And now I can't continue as Alderman any more. And, oh, my poor Will, I've had to sell that little piece of land that your mother and I had hoped would make a gentleman of you."

Will's father came to a halt, overcome with emotion. After sniffing, and wiping his nose on the sleeve of his doublet, he continued. "But we must be brave, Will, and face the facts. I can no longer afford to keep you at school. You must go out and earn your living.

"We have need of good friends now, and a very constant friend is Master Ford, the butcher. Such is his love for this family that he has agreed to have you as his apprentice, to learn the butcher's trade. Seven years, and then … "

Will's father's courage failed him and tears began to run down his cheeks. "Oh, my poor boy, my poor boy," he wailed. "But for your foolish father you could have been a gentleman with a coat of arms, and the respect of all the town, but now … "

Will was appalled. He had no words to say to his blubbering father. He opened the parlour door. "Mother," he said, " I think father needs you."

His mother sighed. "Won't you have some supper, Will?"

Will shook his head. "No thanks, I don't feel hungry, somehow."

The next morning, Will woke early. He lay in bed with the familiar smell of the tanning pools in his nostrils. At least being apprenticed to Master Ford would get him away from this stink. *But perhaps the butcher's would smell as bad,* he thought. *Worse, perhaps, in hot weather?*

But what did the smell matter, he thought bitterly. He was going to be a butcher! No chance now of becoming a scholar at the University of Oxford, of being able to read and picture and imagine to his heart's content, without a Dickon or a Hal or a Jack to pick on him. He pressed his face into the pillow to stop his sobs of bitter despair from waking his brother, Gilbert, fast asleep beside him.

There was a knock at the bedroom door. "Half-past five, son," his mother whispered. "Time to get up for work."

Master Ford's house was very like Will's own, except that where there were tanning pits at the back of Will's house, at the back of the butcher's were animal pens.

"Here we are, Will," said the Master Butcher, with a proud sweep of his arm, "your workplace and your home for the next seven years. When you've completed your apprenticeship, you'll become a journeyman. Then, if you do well, you'll be a fine Master Butcher yourself. Excited, lad?"

Will couldn't answer.

"I'm sure you are. So, here's your first job. We need some cuts of good veal, and this is where they come from!"

Tethered to a stake in the middle of the yard was a calf. It was very much alive.

"Here you are, lad." Master Ford handed him a sharp, broad-bladed knife.

"You want me to – kill it?" Will was aghast.

"That's right, Will," said Master Ford. "It won't jump on the table of its own free will! But don't worry, here comes someone to help you. How are you feeling, Dickon, my boy?"

Coming across the yard was the last person in the world Will wanted to see.

"Better, Father, much better, thank you."

"Poor Dickon's got a bit of a chill," said Master Ford. "Out too late with young rascals like you, up to mischief, eh?" He nudged Will in the ribs.

"Father thought I had better miss school today," said Dickon. "Besides I thought you might need a little advice, Will. Butchering isn't just hacking and chopping."

"It certainly isn't," said Master Ford. "Everything must be done with skill and care, especially the killing. What better place to start, eh, young Will? Don't look so glum, lad. Things may seem bad at home, but you're about to learn a very profitable trade. You'll soon be on the up and up, like me."

Master Ford was interrupted by a thin man in a grimy apron, who came running from the house. "Master Ford, Master Ford! Sir Thomas is here! Sir Thomas Lacy in person! He wishes to order something special for a banquet next Saturday."

"I'll come at once!" said Master Ford. "You see, Will – Sir Thomas Lacy! Up and up! Dickon, you keep an eye on young Will. Give him an apron and show him what to do."

Master Ford bustled back into the house. Dickon handed Will a blood-stained apron, which he tied round his waist. It reached down to his feet.

"Right, Will, this is what you do. Straddle the calf, grip her between your knees, lift up her head and then draw the knife across her throat," said Dickon. "That shouldn't be too difficult for a scholar like yourself."

Will swung his right leg over the tethered calf. It was difficult with the long apron on. As he tried to grip the struggling calf with his knees, Dickon untied the rope from the post.

"Hey! Are you supposed to do that?" shouted Will, as the calf struggled to free itself from his uncertain grip.

Dickon grinned broadly. "One of life's little lessons, Master Scholar-butcher."

The calf, seeing a chance of a reprieve, squirmed backwards out of Will's grasp. Finding itself free, it bolted down the side passage that led into Sheep Street.

"Quick, Will!" cried Dickon. "You'd better catch it or you'll be in deep trouble."

Will turned and ran after the calf, as Dickon began yelling, "Father! Father! He's let it get away!"

Will skidded into Sheep Street, the knife still in his hand. He tried to steady himself, but he lost his footing on the greasy cobbles, tripped over his flapping apron and landed face down in a dung heap outside the front door of the corner house. The knife shot from his grasp and clattered across the cobblestones. It stopped in front of a ragged man crouching against a wall. It was the beggar with the dramatic sores, except that today there were no sores, just a blood-stained bandage covering his eyes.

Will clambered to his feet. He wiped the worst of the filth from his face. His apron was now even more stained. He looked down. Blood was seeping through his torn breeches from two grazed knees.

He hobbled to the end of the road. In the distant water-meadows he could just see the black and white calf cantering towards a large herd of grazing cows and their calves. All of them were black and white.

"What am I going to do?" groaned Will. "I can't go back to Ford's. I can't go back home. I'm ruined – and it's only my first day at work."

"Work! Bah!" said a voice beside him. "Work is for fools and horses!"

It was the beggar, who had pushed up his bandage to watch the progress of the runaway calf.

"There's a good living to be made from dissembling, believe me, young sir," said the beggar, re-arranging the bandages over his eyes. "A bit of paint for sores and blood, a leg tied up here, an arm there. Today I'm blind, tomorrow I may be dumb – but I never go hungry, young master, I never go hungry."

Will didn't reply. He turned and began to trudge along towards the bridge over the river. *Perhaps I should throw myself in the river,* he thought. He leaned on the parapet of the bridge and stared down into the water. No. Things weren't that bad – yet. But how long would he be able to stand being a butcher?

Maybe I should just keep walking, he thought. *I could start a new life in Warwick, or maybe even London.* He looked from the middle of the bridge to his right, then to his left. One road led back into town, to the life he knew. The other led to ... who knew what – excitements and dangers? Which should he take?

The next cart that comes along, thought Will, *I'll flag it down. If they'll give me a lift, I'll take it. I won't care where they're going.* He shut his eyes and waited for the rumble of wheels.

Flipping Fantastic

by Jane Langford

Tristan

I hate the way that I feel right now. I'm not sure how to describe it but I think it's a mixture of sad and bad. How can that be? Well, I feel sad because I'm leaving my old school, and I feel bad because I'm also leaving James.

James is my twin brother. He's much smarter than me. He can do everything. He can dress himself and walk and play football and write with a pen instead of a computer. I would be able to do those things too, if I didn't have a disability.

My mum wouldn't be pleased if she heard me saying 'disability'. She says the word she wants to hear me say is 'ability'.

"I don't know who invented the 'dis' word," she says. "I'm not interested in what you can't do. I'm only interested in what you **can** do."

That's Mum for you, very determined. James isn't like that. He's shy and kind of scared about life. I'm not. Although I'm sad about leaving my old school, I'm excited about my new one. It's a special school to help children get 'able'. Did you like that, Mum? I dropped the 'dis' part of the word.

Anyway, this new school is really cool. It has horses and a huge paddock where you can practise riding! There's a swimming pool so you can go swimming every day. I'm good at swimming. There's a games room which is full of videos, DVDs and computer games. The only problem is that it's a residential school. James is going to a different school and I won't even be there at night for him to tell me what a rubbish day he's had. He'll miss me. I know he will.

James

I can't believe that this is the last week that we'll be here, in this school, together. Tristan and I have always been a team. Wherever he goes, I go. Wherever I go, he goes. I suppose that's not  surprising as I'm always pushing his wheelchair. We're pretty much stuck together and that's the way I like it.

It's the way it's always been, until now. Next term will be different, but I don't want to think about that right now. It's too horrible for words.

Tristan would know the words to describe how horrible it'll be. He's far smarter than me. He can work out maths problems quicker than I can eat a chocolate bar. He always gets 'A's in his homework. He understands how computers work. Yes, he's definitely much smarter than me. How will I cope at my new school without him?

Tristan

Tonight is the school play. It's traditional for Year Six to put on the end-of-year play. It's the last thing we do before we leave, and it's the best thing we do, as well. I've been looking forward to it for ages. We're doing *The Adventures of Tom Sawyer*. I'm Tom! At the end of the play I've got to thank Mr Sewell, our English teacher. He taught us the lines in the play. He's been really great.

I hope the English teacher at my new school is as good as him. We'll be doing drama twice a week, as the school has even got its own drama studio. It's like a little mini-theatre. I can't wait to be performing on the stage. There's plenty of room for wheelchairs and, of course, there's a ramp leading up to it. Here it's really awkward. The only way to get onto the stage is up four steps. Mr Sewell has to carry me while James lifts my wheelchair. Next year, they're having a ramp but it'll be too late for me. I'll be long gone! I'm so excited. I just wish I could stop feeling bad about James.

James

Tonight was the worst night of my life. It was the school play! Talk about embarrassing! The only good thing about my new school is that I won't have to do drama if I don't want to, and believe me – I don't want to!

Tonight was the perfect example of why I hate drama. The hall was absolutely packed with people. Everyone's parents were there. Mum was in the front row. She wanted a good view of Tristan, as he was the star of the show. He was brilliant, of course. I don't know how he manages to learn all those lines. All I had to do was say one measly little line. Could I remember it? No, of course not. One tiny, little line, consisting of just seven words and I got it wrong. Mr Sewell says that nobody noticed but I know that's not true. Jessica Parker laughed at me.

Mum said that Tristan and I were both brilliant, but honestly – am I really expected to fall for that? I was awful. Just because we're twins doesn't mean we have to be good at the same things. I accept that. I think it's about time that Mum did, too.

Mum

Talk about pride! Tonight I thought I was going to burst with it! My two beautiful sons were the stars of the school play. Tristan was wonderful as Tom Sawyer. He spoke his lines so clearly. The woman in the seat behind me said she could hear every word, and Mr Sewell said he was a real 'pro'.

As for James! I could hardly believe it. He actually stood up in front of the whole audience and said his line. He stuttered a bit, but apart from that it was perfect! I never thought I'd see the day when James had the confidence to take part in a school play. He's always been such a shy boy, not at all like his brother.

Tristan, of course, has never been a worry to me. He has always been such an able boy. He may not find it very easy to move his arms and legs, but his mind flows as freely as a freshly oiled cog, and he is so confident.

James, on the other hand, has always been so nervous. I've been really worried about him starting at his new school. It's such a big school, with so many different rooms and subjects and teachers.

I've been worried about how he'll find his way around without Tristan to help him. I thought that if he got lost he would just wander around the corridors for hours, afraid to ask anyone for help. But tonight's performance has given me new confidence in him. He really was wonderful!

Tristan

Last night I was ecstatic. The play put me on a real high. Everyone said I was wonderful as Tom Sawyer. I know I said my lines perfectly and everyone else was brilliant too. The paint on the scenery had actually dried and none of it fell over. The sound system worked and none of the lights shattered with the heat. It was all wonderful.

Today, I feel like a tyre that has burst, totally deflated. Last night was the last time that James and I will be at school together. It's the grand parting of the ways but I'm not sure I'm ready for it. Mum says she is worried about James, but what about me? At least James will have all his friends at his new school. Nearly everyone in our class is going to Highfields. James should be really happy there. But no one is going to Chesterlea Grange with me. It's miles away and I'll only be able to come home at the weekends. I wish that time could have stopped still last night, and we could have stayed at our old school forever.

James

So that's it. Goodbye, Peter Hill Primary. Last night was awful but this morning I feel better. I won't ever have to take part in another school play again as long as I live.

There's another good thing too. For the past six years I've lived in fear of Jessica Parker and her stupid laugh, but now she's moving to a different school and I don't have to worry about seeing her any more. Tristan says that Jessica laughs at me because she wants to attract my attention. Well, I don't want her attention. Maybe at my new school there'll be girls whose attention I won't mind.

Kiara Jones is going to Highfields. She plays football for the County Girls' Under 11s team. With a bit of luck she'll go to the same football practices at Highfields as me. Tristan will be really jealous because he likes Kiara too. She pushed his wheelchair to the refreshment bar at an Under 11s tournament last summer. I couldn't do it because I was playing.

I know that I rely on Tristan but he relies on me too. How will he cope at his new school without me?

Tristan

James seems unusually happy today. How strange, when I am feeling so down. I thought he would be really upset too. The door has finally closed on Peter Hill Primary. James and I were always so happy there. It's the end of a story, the final chapter of a book. We'll probably never go back there again, even to visit.

I won't ever see Mrs Roberts again, either. She's always been our favourite teacher. She takes us for Maths. I mean, she took us for Maths. I wonder who I'll get for Maths at Chesterlea Grange? I hope they're as nice as Mrs Roberts.

It'll be so strange not to be at Peter Hill any more. I'm really going to miss it. I'm going to miss my teachers, my friends and my brother. I'm going to miss the happy familiar way that everything feels. Nothing will be the same at the new school. I feel as if I'm losing something very special. I wonder if everyone feels like this?

James

Tristan is miserable today. He must be tired after the play last night. Mum isn't miserable at all though. She seems strangely pleased with me today. She says I was really confident in the play last night. That's funny! I thought I was a nervous wreck. She obviously didn't know how much I was shaking as I walked onto that stage. My heart was hammering so hard that I thought everyone in the audience would hear it. But maybe Mum's right. Maybe I was more confident. When I was in Year 3, I pretended to be sick on the day of the Christmas concert. Tristan was upset because Mum had to stay with me instead of going to see him in the play. He didn't forgive me for ages. He knew I was scared, not sick, but he didn't tell on me. He protects me. He says that's what big brothers are for. The funny thing is that I'm bigger than him. He's a few minutes older than me, but he is small for his age. I'll know what it feels like to be small when I go to Highfields. I'll be one of the youngest kids instead of one of the oldest like at Peter Hill. Oh no! That last thought was a mistake. It's going to be a disaster. I wish Tristan was coming with me.

Mum

Tristan is a bewildering boy. He's always been such a live wire but for the past two weeks he's been strangely quiet. James has been quiet too, but that's not unusual for him. They both seem to have been depressed since the last day of term. I'm not quite sure why. It _is_ the summer holidays after all. Perhaps it was a mistake to choose different secondary schools for them. They're very different children but they're still twins. It's hard for the rest of us to understand quite how they feel. I must ask them again if this is what they really want. I can't let them spend the rest of the summer holidays looking as if they've won the Lottery, then lost the ticket down a drain!

Tristan

Mum just asked me if I really want to go to Chesterlea Grange! Is she joking? Of course I don't want to! I want to go back to Peter Hill. It's safe there, and friendly and everybody knows me. The thing is, when I went to see Chesterlea Grange on the Open Day, it seemed so much fun. I liked the horse-riding, swimming and wheelchair games best. Every summer they hold an event like the Paralympics. They have archery contests, wheelie marathons and basketball tournaments. I've never had the chance to take part in sports like that.

James has always been the one in our family who's good at sports. I'd really like it if it was me for a change.

Now I'm just confused! I don't know what to think. I told Mum that I didn't want to go to Chesterlea Grange any more. What have I done? I bet that right now she is fixing for me to go to Highfields with James!

Mum

Words fail me! Tristan doesn't want to go to Chesterlea Grange after all. What on earth am I going to do?

James

I am so relieved! Tristan has just told Mum that he doesn't want to go to Chesterlea after all. That means he will be coming to Highfields with me. Thank goodness for that! I don't know how I would have managed without him. I was already thinking up a million excuses not to go to school on the first day. I've thought of every illness from bubonic plague to yellow fever. Somehow I don't think that Mum would have believed any of them!

I know that Highfields probably won't be half as bad as I think but I'm still very glad that Tristan will be there with me. He can look after me and I can look after him. I can help him with his wheelchair up all the ramps in the corridors and I can hold back the automatic doors when they start to close too soon. I can make sure that he can get to the toilet when he needs to, and I can tell the teacher what he can and can't do in PE.

Hang on a minute! That's not right! Mum said the best thing about Chesterlea Grange was that Tristan wouldn't have anybody to do all those things for him. "I know you're clever and confident," she said to Tristan when we first talked about him going away to school, "but you still rely on other people to do too much for you and it's time you stood on your own two feet!"

Stand on his own two feet!! Tristan thought that was hilarious. The next best thing about Chesterlea Grange is all those great games and computer equipment that they have. Tristan was really excited about those. So what's happened? Why has he changed his mind? I've been so busy thinking about all the problems that I might have at Highfields that I haven't taken much notice of Tristan, even though he's been a terrible grump lately. Perhaps it's time I talked to him. If he won't tell me what's wrong, then he won't tell anyone.

Tristan

OK, I've really blown it! James has just talked to me about not going to Chesterlea Grange anymore. But I know that I do want to go now, I really do. Even if I hadn't already changed my mind, James reminded me about all the great things that we saw when we visited the school, and how friendly the staff were. The more we talked, the more certain I became that I would never forgive myself if I didn't go. It's such a marvellous place. I'd really be missing out if I didn't go there. I've just been a bit nervous about it, that's all. Me, nervous! That's a first!

At least all this has taught me one thing. I understand now how James feels about a lot of things. I've never really worried about anything before but I've managed to get into quite a state about this school thing.

James is such a pest! I wish he didn't know me quite so well. If he hadn't talked to me I might still have stuck with my decision not to go to Chesterlea. But I'm not going to stick with it. How can I tell Mum?

James

Me and my big mouth! Why did I ever go and talk to Tristan about his new school? He's changed his mind again. He's gone to tell Mum that he just had a bad case of the collywobbles, and that he does want to go to Chesterlea Grange after all.

I must be mad for helping to persuade him. Now I've got to face Highfields all on my own. What a nightmare!

Tristan

Phew, what a relief! Mum doesn't mind that I've changed my mind again. James does though. I can see that old scared look back in his eyes. What can I do to make him feel better? I bet he's feeling just as scared about Highfields as I was about Chesterlea Grange. In fact, knowing James, he probably feels twice as bad. I must talk to him and see what I can do. James doesn't want me to leave him. I know he doesn't.

Mum

Tomorrow is the first day of the new term. Both my boys are nervous. That's to be expected. But they're also excited. Both of them are looking forward to the new start.

I'm so proud of them. James helped Tristan to realise that he did want to go to Chesterlea Grange after all. Tristan helped James to look forward to going to Highfields by making sure that he had a special friend to help him through the first few days. How did he do that? He phoned Kiara Jones, of course. Apparently he made friends with her at an Under 11s tournament. It seems that James wanted to make friends with her, too!!

James

Highfields is brilliant. Lots of my old friends are there and I've made loads of new friends too. Kiara and I have both been chosen for the football teams that we tried for. I can't wait to see Tristan at the weekend to tell him all about it!

Tristan

James, my old mate. There's only one way to describe Chesterlea Grange.

Flipping fantastic!

Mani's Walk-Alone
by William Bedford

Chapter One

"In the beginning, the world was asleep," said the Elder. "The world was emptiness, and silence and darkness. Nothing moved."

The Elder stood very still beside the flames of the fire. His body was decorated with white and ochre paint, shining in the red glow of the fire. He held his mulga-wood hunting spear firmly in his right hand.

"In the beginning," the Elder went on, "the Ancestors travelled the unshaped world, creating everything that lives. The Emu Ancestor created the emu. The Eucalyptus Tree Ancestor created the eucalyptus tree. The Brolga Bird Ancestor created the brolga bird."

The men who had gathered around the fire grunted their agreement. Smoke filled Mani's eyes and made them water but he could still see his father seated with the other men. His father looked away, unwilling to embarrass him.

"That was the time we call the Dreamtime," the Elder continued after a long silence. "The Dreamtime, when our Ancestors created dingoes and kangaroos, honey-ants and the flight of the lyre bird, rivers, and the red sand of the desert. The Dreamtime, when our Ancestors made the world and the ways of our tribe."

Abruptly, the Elder lifted his hunting spear and all the men around the fire shouted and raised their own spears. When at last the Elder had finished speaking, the rhythmic clicking of boomerangs being banged together, the drone of didgeridoos and the clapping of hands erupted into the stillness of the night air. The dancing would go on until dawn. All the men of the tribe joined in the dancing. There were no women allowed at the ritual. This corroboree was for the beginning of Mani's walk-alone.

Chapter Two

Mani walked from the corroboree in the hour before dawn. The sky was black, glittering with necklaces of stars. The desert was an endless pit of emptiness. The clicking of the boomerangs went on.

Mani was fourteen years old. He was a tall, thin boy, his crinkly hair as dark as his satiny skin, his eyes blue-black and full of laughter. He wore emu feathers in his hair, and moistened ochre streaked his face and chest. He carried the black ceremonial boomerang made of hard mulga-wood, and his hunting spear. He lived with his kin on ancestral lands west of Tennant Creek, in the red-sand heart of the Tanami Desert. His people were the Bindaboo.

Mani's life had been lived by the laws of his tribe. There was a time to be born and a time to leave the mother; there was a time to travel with the tribe and a time to walk-alone; a time for hunting and a time to die. Among all the Aborigine tribes, Bindaboo boys were the only ones who went walk-alone.

For Mani, the time had come to walk-alone. He could walk wherever he wished, but he had to complete his journey before the coming of the rains. The walk-alone, from one group of water-holes to another, would take many moons to complete. He could carry no water. He had to complete the journey alone and without help. When his walk-alone was completed, he would be a man in his tribe.

His father was waiting for him at the edge of the desert. He was not supposed to leave the fire and speak to Mani but he did not always follow the rules. As a young hunter, he had been a rebel.

"You are on your way then, Mani," he said solemnly.

"You shouldn't be here, Father."

"I can wish my own son good fortune on his walk-alone, can't I?"

Mani breathed the red sands of the desert. He thought about his mother and sisters, and his little brother Nym, who was always getting into trouble and upsetting the Elders with his jokes and adventures.

"I will miss Nym," Mani said.

"I will watch over him," Mani's father replied, and they both grinned. Mani was thinking that, although Nym was only nine years old, he would take more looking after than his father could manage.

"You will be a man soon, Mani,"
his father said.

"When I have completed my walk-alone."

"Like our Ancestors who created the world,"
his father nodded. "In the Dreamtime, they went
walk-alone. It is one of the laws of our tribe."

"You don't always obey the laws, Father," Mani
pointed out.

His father grinned. "This one is a good law. It
will teach you to be a man."

"Like you," Mani said simply.

"Well, not entirely like me, maybe. You will be
yourself." Mani recognised the wisdom in his
words.

"I will walk with you in my heart," his father
said in farewell.

"That would be good," Mani smiled, and he
stepped into the darkness of the desert.

Chapter Three

Mani walked into the dawn. The sun was rising behind him. Blackness lay ahead. He walked easily, his naked feet touching the ground lightly. His tribe had hunted this desert for thousands of years. Their land was a stony land, broken by rivers and waterholes, mountains and grassy plains, lakes and red sands.

Slowly, the desert grew out of the darkness. There was mile after mile of shimmering ridge and dune, salt-pan and iron-rock, and glaring sand. The clicking of the boomerangs still sounded in Mani's head but now there was another sound.

He halted and stood on one leg, listening to the desert, the harsh iron-rock. He was miles from his home now, from his father and from the Elders of the tribe, but he knew he was being followed.

Were the Ancestors following him on his walk-alone? That could not be. The Ancestors had long ago gone back to sleep. Was it the night-hunting dingoes, with their sharp teeth and dismal howls? The dingoes would follow a man until he collapsed into the red dust and then they would feast. But they were night hunters and would be gone by now. Mani walked on into the heat.

Many hours later, in the heat of midday, he came across a straggle of eucalyptus trees. In the shelter of the trees he found a cluster of yams, buried among their flowers and leaves. He dug them out, then dug down into the sand and found water. Mani drank slowly, while eating the sweet, fat yams.

After his rest, he strode on towards the pale brown hills that climbed out of the heat-haze above the shimmering sand. The tallest hill was called the 'hill-that-fell-out-of-the-sky'. The desert stretched around him, dancing in the heat and reddened by the blistering sun. Mani was excited to be on his own at last.

Chapter Four

It was twilight when Mani reached the hills. He could smell water and quickly found a stream. Fireflies hovered as Mani waded into the water. Holding his hunting spear high three times, he stabbed and caught three fat fish.

He made a fire among the rocks and collected yacca wood for the flames. The wood was dry and brittle from the dry season. The rains would come later, after Mani had finished his walk-alone.

He wrapped the fish in eucalyptus leaves and baked them among hot stones in the fire. The smoke rose and smelled sweet from the flesh of the fish. There were no sounds except the running stream and the crackling fire.

Suddenly, Mani heard footsteps. He spun round in his alarm and stared into the darkness. Was it a bush ghost, come to fetch him to the land of the dead? Mani stood, gripping his spear, trying to be brave. He could feel his heart racing with fright.

The figure who stepped from the eucalyptus trees was tall and slim like Mani, but younger.

"Is that you, Mani?" the figure called.

Mani stared at his little brother in disbelief. Had Nym died and come to him as a bush ghost? But he seemed real. Also, ghosts weren't nervous, and Nym looked frightened.

"What are you doing here?" Mani shouted
angrily.

Nym started to say, "I'm sorry, Mani," but was
stopped by the fury in his brother's face.

"Sorry!" Mani raged, clutching his spear as
though he might hurl it straight at his brother.

Nym hung his head. "I missed you," he said.
"I wanted to come with you."

Mani stood in silence for a long time, his fingers tight around his spear. It was Nym in the desert, not an Ancestor. Little brother Nym, who was nine years old and followed him everywhere, and who was always getting into trouble.

Abruptly, Mani sat down beside the fire and the baking fish. He was too shocked to know what to say.

Nym came shyly to the fire. He said nothing, because he had understood the terrible thing he had done. He had prevented his brother from going on his walk-alone. The Elders would never forgive him and they would punish Mani. He would not become a man. They ate in silence, then lay down beside the fire.

Mani stared up at the stars. He felt darkness moving into his mind but there was nothing he could do. Nym would be eaten by dingoes if Mani left him in the desert. But with Nym, Mani would not be able to complete his walk-alone. He would fail to become a man. There would be no place for him in the tribe. Mani closed his eyes and went to sleep. There were no dreams from the Ancestors.

Chapter Five

With the dawn, Mani and Nym woke instantly. They heard the flip-flap-flip of the flying foxes and then the howl of the dingoes out in the desert. A wombat foraged through the underscrub searching for roots. The fireflies became pale and then went out like snuffed candles. Mani and Nym ate the last of the fish and drank water from the stream.

"I can go back alone," Nym said.

"Shut up."

"But Mani ... "

"I must take you back. It is my responsibility."

"I got here by myself," Nym protested, proud of his long march through the red desert. "They won't blame you, Mani," he added hopefully. "Only a fool would follow you on your walk-alone."

"Then I should have known I had a fool for a brother," Mani said curtly.

Nym stood up, frightened. He had never seen his brother so angry. He walked away and looked at the water. A grey light was climbing from the east.

Nym wished he had not come but he did not know what to do. He could go off into the bush when Mani wasn't looking but he knew Mani would follow him. Mani was already a good tracker. Nym stared hopelessly at the rising sun.

Then suddenly, he felt a pain in his leg, then another and another. Huge jumping ants were attacking him, their bites tearing at his skin. Nym ran to the stream and plunged into the water, yelling with the pain. He went under the water and then, as he climbed out, he slipped and fell.

Mani watched his brother's antics. How could he be fooling around at such a time? Then he realised Nym was shouting with pain. He ran to his brother's side. Nym had wrenched his ankle and it was already swelling. Now, even walking home would be difficult. Nym might not make it!

"Can you be any more of a nuisance?" Mani said furiously. "I ought to leave you for the dingoes. They would enjoy a good meal."

Mani poured water onto Nym's swollen ankle and wrapped it in eucalyptus leaves. Nym was groaning with the pain. Mani searched his brother's eyes for the spirit of death and felt frightened. If the spirit of death had come searching for Nym, there would be nothing Mani could do. But the spirit of death was not in his brother's eyes. Nym was alive and hurting, and cross with himself for falling on the rocks.

"I can't walk," he said angrily. Mani nodded.

"I am going to die," Nym announced.

"No, you're not," insisted Mani. "You are in a lot of trouble but you are not going to die. The spirit of death doesn't want you."

On the top branch of a mulga-wood tree, a kookaburra sent up its raucous flow of laughter, shattering the calm of the morning. Mani wondered if the kookaburra bird was laughing at them, but decided it was probably just annoyed because they had disturbed the frogs and snakes which were its usual breakfast.

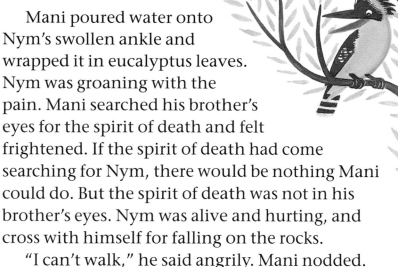

Mani made sure his brother was comfortable and then went to find food. He caught a baby wallaby and brought it back to the camp. He shared some honey-ants with Nym and then set about waking the fire.

When the wallaby was cooking, Mani went off to collect more yacca wood for the fire. Nym was sleeping when he returned. Mani poured fresh cold water onto the eucalyptus leaves around Nym's swollen ankle, and laughed when Nym woke from his sleep with a startled protest. Despite his anger, Mani could not help enjoying his brother's company. Nobody could stay cross with Nym for long.

They shared more honey-ants and then Mani went to look at 'the-hill-that-fell-out-of-the-sky'. If he had been alone, he would have climbed the hill to walk where the Ancestors had walked. On a walk-alone, a boy could meet his soul spirit, but Mani could not leave Nym now. There were wild cats in the bush, as well as dingoes, and they would enjoy eating his little brother. When it was time for the boys to eat, Mani took the wallaby from the fire and they ate the tender flesh. The day passed slowly with Nym fitfully sleeping and Mani standing guard over him.

By the end of the second day, Nym's ankle was not so swollen and he tried to walk, leaning on Mani's shoulder.

"They will be searching for you," Mani said, as they stumbled along together.

"For a thrashing," Nym said woefully.

Mani said nothing. He felt the great sadness return and settle on his heart.

Nym saw the sadness in his brother's eyes. He knew that he had put it there and he felt his own eyes wet with salty tears.

"I'm sorry, Mani," he said in a small voice. Mani shrugged and smiled. He knew his little brother was sorry and, when they got back, the Elders and his father would make sure he was even more sorry. Mani didn't envy Nym at all.

Chapter Six

They set off on the third morning,
taking a different way back across the desert.
They could not walk over their own footsteps
in case they disturbed any bush ghost who
might be following them.

As Mani and Nym walked, the bush beyond
the hills shone like a rainbow: jade and
emerald, white and red, crimson, scarlet and
gold. They passed giant eucalyptus trees, their
trunks white as skeletons, their leaves
shrivelling in the blazing sun. They saw the
iron-bark trees which never die, and
mellowbane, and tawny leopard trees.

The trees were swarming with birds:
cockatoos with yellow tails, gang-gangs
dangling upside down, budgerigars flitting
madly from tree to tree. Bustards were scratching
and pecking the ground below. A bustard
chick would be tender and plump enough
to eat later when they were hungry.

Mani stood motionless on one leg,
waiting for one to stray close enough.
When a chick pecked at his foot, he
snatched it up and stuffed it in
his pouch. He was proud of
his speed and skill.

Nym walked painfully slowly. It would take them two days to make the journey home, travelling at this pace, but there was no need for haste. They had drunk plenty of water before leaving the hills, and eaten a good breakfast of fish and quondong, the red fruit that was sweet and juicy and thirst-quenching. Mani had several of the fruits in his pouch and he knew where he could find water.

In the heat of the day, they found shelter among some rocks. Nym rested while Mani made a fire. There was little yacca wood in this part of the desert but he found enough. He prepared the chick bustard and got it roasting, then he dug down into the sand for water.

They ate more of the quondong fruit, finished half the bustard and drank some water before setting out again.

It was not easy walking and, with Nym leaning on his arm, Mani became more and more tired. Their feet stirred up clouds of fine red dust, and there was no water to be found now. A shimmering haze of redness stretched before them. Mani felt weak and weary. He pushed aside the thought that the spirit of death had in truth come searching for him, not for his brother.

Chapter Seven

The two boys walked on. The sun dropped lower in the sky, which glowed rose and gold. At the first breath of the sunset wind, they made camp. There was no water but the quondong quenched their thirst and they were too tired to eat what was left of the bustard.

Out of the dusk came flying ants. A dingo howled across the desert. Mani stirred the fire to keep the ants away, and to frighten the dingoes.

"Thank you, Mani," Nym said as they lay beside the fire.

Mani reached out his hand and touched his brother's shoulder. "We will reach home tomorrow," he promised.

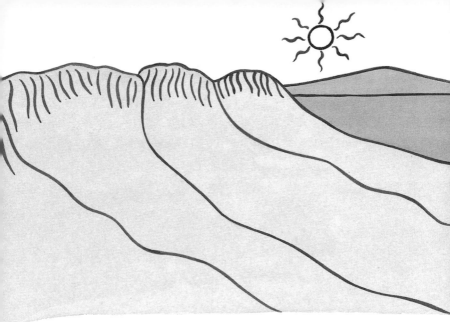

Dawn brought wreaths of mist as the heat of the sun warmed the dew-wet rocks, making them steam like the earth after summer rain. Mani and Nym staggered to their feet. They were weary and hungry.

A great tiredness seemed to be dragging them down into the ground but they knew that would mean death. They set out walking again, their eyes blinded by the sun, the heat a throbbing furnace inside their minds. They had not walked far when Nym's legs folded beneath him.

Without saying anything, Mani lifted his brother onto his back and staggered on. In his weariness, he wondered again whether the spirit of death had been looking for him all this time. It must not find him before he got Nym safely home.

Chapter Eight

The Elders gathered around the fire and listened solemnly to Mani's tale. Some of them were frowning. Others did not look at Mani at all, but stared into the fire. Mani was ashamed and spoke in a low voice.

When Mani had told his tale, he limped away from the firelight and went back to his mother and sisters. The brothers had slept for most of the day, waiting for the Elders to send for them. Nym was still fast asleep. His feet were blistered from the walk but he would recover after a long sleep.

Mani was not sure that he would ever be all right.

Mani's father came for him as the crescent moon hung at the top of the sky like a silver boomerang. They walked together to the edge of the desert. A dingo howled far away and another answered, their cries echoing across the darkness.

"I did not know what to do," Mani confessed.

His father nodded solemnly. "I'm not surprised. I don't know what to do about Nym myself, and I am his father."

Mani laughed, and then felt sad. "But I did not complete my walk-alone," he whispered, hardly able to speak the words. "I have done a great wrong."

There was a silence. The desert rustled in the darkness. The moon was cold and far away.

"No," Mani's father said softly. "Nothing you have done has been wrong."

Mani gulped. He fought back the tears in his eyes. "I did not complete my walk-alone," he said again, the tears wetting his cheeks. "I will not be a man now."

His father turned and put his hand on Mani's arm. "You are already a man," he said quietly.

Together, they walked back to the fire where the Elders were beginning the celebration corroboree. Already the clicking of the boomerangs and the hum of the didgeridoos filled the darkness. Mani walked proudly with his father into the firelight. They stood shoulder to shoulder as the Elders greeted them with raised spears.